We would like to dedicate this story to all children who conquered their fears by receiving their vaccinations. We salute you!

A Letter to Parents:

Vaccinations are not fun, but they are extremely important. During the first few weeks of life, children have some protection against illness due to the antibodies (disease fighting agents) that were passed down from mother to child. Since a child's body may not be strong enough to fight off these dangerous diseases alone AND many of these illnesses are very contagious, getting your child vaccinated is extremely important! Many children have died or experienced life-long consequences from diseases like polio, measles, and pneumonia before vaccines were routinely administered to kids. Thankfully, vaccinations have helped to make these diseases less common and less life-threatening.

How do vaccines work?

Vaccines introduce a form of the disease-causing agent, an antigen, to the body. These antigens are either weakened or killed germs or viruses. When a person is exposed to these antigens in a vaccine, they cause the body to make the necessary equipment, also known as antibodies, to fight against the actual disease. So, if a child is exposed to the disease in the environment, he/she already has the necessary "equipment" to fight off the illness and help prevent it from causing serious consequences.

Should I be worried about vaccinating my child?

Vaccines not only protect your child, but they also protect children too young to receive vaccinations, the community, and future generations. In recent years, there have been many myths that have made some parents concerned about the safety of giving vaccinations to their children. The most notable myth is that vaccinations are linked with autism. The Institute of Medicine, the American Academy of Pediatrics, and the CDC have conducted their own research into the safety of vaccinations and have found no connection between vaccinations and autism in children. Unfortunately, recent failure to provide children with the recommended vaccinations has resulted in actual outbreaks of these diseases, such as measles. Parents have more reason to fear the diseases the vaccines can prevent rather than the myths. Further reading on vaccine safety is available from the Centers for Disease Control and Prevention (CDC), the American Academy of Pediatrics, and the Immunization Action Coalition. In contrast to these myths, the most common side effects of vaccines are muscle soreness and a mild fever.

What vaccinations should my child receive?

The CDC keeps full, up-to-date, printable vaccination schedules on its website under "Immunization Schedules" (www.cdc.gov/vaccines/schedules). These schedules tell when certain vaccinations are due and why they are important. We hope that this book helps to take some of the "sting" out of vaccinations by explaining to kids how vaccines help to keep them healthy!

1. Centers for Disease Control and Prevention website: www.cdc.gov. Updated February 2015.
2. American Academy of Pediatrics website: www.aap.org. Updated December 2009.
3. Advisory Committee on Immunizations Practices website: www.cdc.gov/vaccines/acip. Updated February 2015.

This is little Max Greene when he was a flu vaccine in the making!

The youngest of the Greenes, growing into a big shot was his for the taking.

He dreamt of the day when he would awake with a jerk,

blink his eyes, uncap his needle, and get to work.

Papa
Polio

Mama
Meningitis

Max

So he polished his needle and kept it real clean,

and learned all the rules from his elder vaccines.

Then finally one day his dad told him to prepare,

for this was the year he would become part of healthcare.

So as the day neared, Max was delighted.

He couldn't wait to make kids more excited.

He saw signs that said, "GET YOUR BACK-TO-SCHOOL SHOTS!"

and waited outside to see the sweet, happy tots.

But when they came out their smiles were turned down.

Max wondered, "What makes these little ones frown?

They've done well and should be smiling," he said with surprise.

But instead, the children left with tears in their eyes.

Max said, "I know what it is! They're unhappy because school starts soon!

They'd rather spend the day eating ice cream, playing, or watching cartoons.

Instead they are at the doctor's office wishing they were done.

But don't worry kids, I'll think of something to make it more fun."

So Max thought of a plan and knew who would come in handy.

He called his three friends Chipper, Bandi Boo-Boo, and Sandy.

Chipper was a sticker,

Sandy was a sugar candy,

and Bandi Boo-Boo was a band-aid.

Max said. "Kids aren't happy with shots! They need something fun to do.

There needs to be someone to make the kids laugh. Chipper, that will be you.

Then they need a treat, something sugary and sweet,

Sandy, give them a sugar rush they can't wait to eat.

They are missing their favorite cartoons, Bandi this is where you come on board,

Show them their favorite characters and stick right on their arm, like an award."

Chipper, excited about the plan, asked with glee,

"What about you, Max? What are you going to be?"

"I'll give them their shots, which is no problem you see.

They just need to have fun; that's why you are helping me."

Together they cheered, "We'll be every parent's dream!

We will be known as The Vaccine Team!"

So Max left to get some rest for tomorrow's big day

after he thanked his friends for helping out in such a huge way.

When Max left, Bandi said to Chipper and Sandy,

"Guys, I know why kids aren't happy.

I've been in the doctor's offices to learn and explore.

They don't like shots because they sting and make them sore."

Chipper said, "It will break Max's heart if he knows why these kids cry."

"Well, we shouldn't hurt his feelings," said Sandy sweet as pie.

"So let's do our best to make these kids laugh and smile.

Max won't have to know a thing. Trust me, it will be worthwhile."

So all three agreed and the next day they arrived at their first appointment.

As the doctor was getting Max ready, his friends saw the kids' disappointment.

They're more nervous than I thought they'd be," Chipper noted, shaking his head.

"We have to introduce ourselves and let them know it will be okay," Sandy said.

Chipper was first. "I'm Chipper the Sticker! Shots can be a kicker!
But I'm here to cheer you up and make the tears leave quicker."
Sandy followed, "I'm Sandy the Sugar Candy! I know shots can hurt,
but I'll give you some dessert."
"And I'm Bandi Boo-Boo! I have bright pictures and I stick to your arm
where they gave you that shot that keeps you from harm."

When Max came back in and didn't see any tears,

he thought his plan had worked and it put him in good cheer.

"**HELLO!**" Max burst,

"I love to give shots! Who wants to go first?"

To Max's surprise, there was no more cheer

and not one person volunteered.

The kids were merry with the rest of the clan,

but when it came to Max, they weren't his biggest fan.

was then Max realized the problem wasn't kids having fun; it was him all along.

"How could I have missed the signs? It is clear this is not where I belong.

I don't want to make the kids sad. I want to prevent them from getting sick.

To do that, I have to get the vaccine into their bodies. It's just a little prick."

That's when something inside Max snapped,

and he decided that his needle must be capped.

From that day forward, Max decided to hide.

He had given up hope but at least he had tried.

Meanwhile, the flu season came ever near

and a new virus was coming to town as it did every year.

When it arrived, it made people sick and people sneeze,

with noses runny and feeling chills down to their knees.

The flu from one person can spread to another:

mom, dad, sister, or brother.

Those who have the flu and sneeze on their hands,

what they touch next is where the virus lands.

The best defense wasn't to stop it from coming to town.

It was to make the kids stronger so they'd take the virus down.

The only way to do that was to be vaccinated,

but as Max knew, this was one thing all kids hated.

Chipper, Bandi, and Sandy made kids happy, but they weren't providing protection.

They needed Max to help keep the kids healthy and safe from infection.

"We need another plan. It was wrong for me to keep the truth from Max.

We need to get him back and tell the children the real facts."

"How can we get Max back and save the children?" Sandy asked with worry.

"I have an idea," said Chipper, "but we will have to hurry."

Chipper called Max in a panic. "It's an emergency, Max. You have to come back!

The kids are in danger. The flu virus has come and it's on the attack."

Caring deeply for the kids as he did, Max rushed over forgetting about his fear.

When he arrived, he could hear his friends speaking to the kids loud and clear.

Chipper was first. "I'm Chipper the Sticker! Boy, that shot can be a kicker,

but Max is a great guy and wants to make you healthier, not sicker."

Then Sandy. "I'm Sandy the Sugar Candy! I know that shot might not be fun,

but it's protecting you in the long run."

Then Bandi. "I'm Bandi Boo-Boo! When the shot leaves behind a boo-boo,

it's to show other kids that you're brave and they can do it too."

Max was so touched to realize what he meant to his friends and his community.

Bandi rushed over. "Max, you're the only one who can give these kids immunity."

Max then knew what he had to do,

he uncapped his needle and rejoined the crew.

The Vaccine Team was back together at last!

One by one they helped kids stay healthy until the flu season passed.

"We're happy you got your vaccine, but just to be clear,

make sure you stop by to see us next year!"

Acknowledgments

We would like to extend a special thanks to Dr. Erin Albert, Professor Angela Lupton, Dr. Stephanie Fernhaber, Professor Lisa Hines, and Dr. Emily Papineau for being the foundation through which this book was possible. We would also like to express our sincerest gratitude to our family, friends, and readers for their continual support, feedback, and encouragement throughout this process.

About the Authors and Illustrators

Emily Ellsworth is a sixth year pharmacy student currently undergoing her advanced practice rotations to complete her degree. Emily was interested in writing this children's book because she has a passion for improving public health by increasing the education on vaccinations. In her free time, Emily enjoys discovering new recipes, reading, and spending time with family and friends. Emily enjoys volunteering at an elderly daycare center located by Butler University's campus and would like to continue working with the elderly upon graduation.

Anissa Hakim's interest in the sciences influenced her to begin as a Pharmacy major but she soon switched to Elementary Education as she continued to discover and grow into herself as a young adult. Following her passion for reading and learning, as well as her childhood dream of becoming an author and illustrator, she joined this project to educate children. In combination with her experiences in healthcare, all of these factors fueled her hope of encouraging children to tackle their fear of shots and inform them in an encouraging way to help them see the benefits of being brave and getting their vaccinations.

Terri Newman is a sixth year College of Pharmacy student. For her, the rewarding part about her pharmacy curriculum was the ability to be a positive influence in the health and wellness of patients, friends, and family. Inspired by the opportunity to raise health awareness in children and combine her passion for creativity with her science-based background, she knew she had to be a part of this project. With pastimes that include photography, poetry, and blogging, Terri has contributed a well-rounded skillset to this project. Her future aspirations include working in the pharmaceutical industry to aid in the development and utilization of innovative and safe medications.

Katrina Rodriguez is an Elementary Education major with a licensure in Early Childhood. She decided to pursue working with young children after she attended an education conference in Reggio Emilia, Italy. She will be graduating in May 2015. After graduation she plans to work in a Reggio-Inspired early childhood classroom. Katrina was inspired to join the project because she has a passion for children's literature and feels strongly about educating young children. Katrina hopes that after children read this book, they will feel confident and informed when receiving their vaccinations.

Matt Speer is pursuing B.S. degrees in both Finance and Entrepreneurship & Innovation. He will graduate in May of 2015. He has diverse business experience, including numerous internships during his time at Butler. Matt was recently selected as an Orr Fellow and will start working at Bluebridge Digital in June of 2015. In the meantime, Matt acts as the Senior Class Treasurer at Butler University. Matt is also working with fellow team member Andres Pena as a co-founder of an app, called rippl, which will help streamline social giving for both the everyday giver and any non-profit organization across the United States. The beta version of the app will be available on the App Store after February 1, 2015 and will feature 10 non-profits across the Midwest!

Andres Peña was born in Barranquilla, Colombia. He is currently working on achieving a double major in Marketing and Entrepreneurship through Butler University's College of Business. Andres has held several leadership roles and has started his own app company with fellow project team member, Matt Speer. Other groups he is involved in include Sigma Nu Fraternity and the Butler American Marketing Association. Andres was the Social Chair for the Epsilon Mu Chapter of Sigma Nu Fraternity. In this role, he planned the house's social events and worked to improve chapter relations with sororities.

Mara Olson is a modern day Renaissance woman pursuing a BS degree in Biology along with minors in Neuroscience, Chemistry, Spanish, and Art & Design. Mara is also a three-time NCAA Division I All-American in cross-country and track, sporting the Butler blue in races nationwide. Her wide range of interests has led to diverse experiences, including preclinical research of neurodegenerative disorders and academic support for Latino students in the Indianapolis community. Mara is from St. Louis Park, Minnesota, and expects to attend medical school after graduating this spring.